LiStEH To Me!

WINNING SHORT STORIES
WRITTEN BY TEENAGERS

EDITED BY WENDY COOLING

Collins

An imprint of HarperCollins*Publishers*

Winning stories from a national writing competition to celebrate the launch of *Centuries of Stories*, edited by Wendy Cooling.

First published in paperback by Collins in 2000
Collins is an imprint of HarperCollins*Publishers* Ltd
77-85 Fulham Palace Road, Hammersmith, London W6 8JB

1 3 5 7 9 8 6 4 2

Collection copyright © Collins 2000
Individual stories © individual authors as credited

ISBN 0 00 675536 4

The editor and authors assert the moral right to be
identified as the editor and authors of the work.

Printed and bound in Great Britain by
Omnia Books Limited, Glasgow

Contents

Introduction

Thank you to the writers of these stories and to all the young people who submitted work for the *Centuries of Stories* short-story writing competition. Choosing just fourteen was not easy as every story showed imagination and creative thinking, as well as strongly developing writing skills.

The stories in this anthology represent the work of young writers of the twenty-first century. They write of tough things: death, old age, the future and the unexpected. There are fantasy stories as well as stories of love and horror, and tales of alchemy and other magic. To this mix is added more than a touch of humour, and the result is a collection of writing that reflects the ideas, reading interests and writing skills of young people. *Centuries of Stories* contains a story set in each of the last twenty centuries and so it celebrates the last 2000 years; the writers are the best award-winning contemporary authors. *Listen to Me*! is another celebration, one that looks to the future, one for all young people to read, enjoy and then, I hope, to write on!

Wendy Cooling

Listen To Me!

BY JENNY BYWATER

The last thing I remember is the echo of that terrible scream. I think it came from Mum. I open my eyes slowly. There are lots of bright lights. Lots of flashing lights. But no sound. That's the strange thing. There is no sound anywhere. Not even the normal sounds of the wind in the trees, or the rain splashing on to the pavement. I know it's raining. I can feel the water soaking through my clothes.

Now I can see clearly. Even though the light still hurts my eyes, the mist that covered them a moment ago has disappeared. There are people everywhere; some with their mouths wide open. They're shouting with no sound. It's eerie. Maybe the crash affected my hearing. Maybe I'm deaf.

I think about Mum again. I have to find her. I try to sit up slowly, and am overwhelmed by this wave of incredible pain and dizziness. Then I hear a loud buzzing sound in my ear. Like a huge, angry bee is trapped in there. I have one hell of a headache. Gingerly I get to my feet. As I stand my vision blurs, and I stay there, wobbling for a moment until it clears again. I take a step forward, towards the light. I must have been thrown clear when we collided. I am lucky to be alive.

I try to move more quickly, but each step jars my whole body, resulting in almost unbearable agony. As I reach the scene of the crash, I see my mother being loaded into the back of an ambulance. Her mouth is open, and she's clawing at the blanket around her, while desperate tears flood her face.

Suddenly all the sounds rush back, invading my mind. Filling it with pain. I catch the last part of Mum's speech – 'NO!'

I run, and reach the ambulance just before they close the doors behind her. I slip inside and crouch beside the stretcher. I think Mum's passed out. She's just lying there. She looks a lot older than I remember. And sad. No, worse than that: desolate. It's as if she has lost the most important thing in her whole life. The way she looked when Dad died. A feeling of panic rushes through my veins. What if she's dying? I bang on the back of the driver's seat and yell, 'Hurry up! For God's sake, hurry up! Please!'

I turn back to Mum and lay my head on her chest, like I used to do when I was about five and scared of some monster or shadow. I hear her heart beating, and for some reason this fills me with sadness, and I too begin to cry softly. I don't know why I cry now. It's like there's suddenly a barrier between us that I can't cross. I can't reach her any more.

The ambulance pulls to a halt and the doors open. The men rush in, and I squash myself against the side of the van, so I'm not in the way. They wheel Mum out, and she regains consciousness. She starts screaming, 'My baby! I want my baby! I want my Roxy!'

Roxy. That's me. She named me Roxanne,

after her favourite song. I've always hated it, but now I'm glad to hear it. It proves she's alive. She wants me. I step out of the ambulance and follow the men wheeling her into the hospital. I call out, 'It's me, Mum! I'm here, don't worry!' I don't think she hears me, what with all the shouting and noise around here.

I walk into the hospital with them and sit down as they push her into what I assume is an operating room. I am left alone. There's a coffee machine fixed on to the wall a few feet away, and I get up and walk over to it, searching my pocket for some change. I have about £1. I press the button for coffee with milk, but nothing happens. I try again, but the button doesn't even move. Maybe it's jammed. I press the button for black coffee, but that one's jammed too. I press all of them, one after the other, as hard as I can, but nothing happens. The machine's broken, and it's eaten all my money.

I remember a lot of things. In all of them, I am lost or scared or alone, and Mum finds me, or hugs me, or makes me smile.

I think I fall asleep, because the next thing I know, I am waking up to sunlight streaming through the window, and the quiet sobs of my mother. She's in bed and the curtains are pulled around us. I sit up, my headache is gone. I lean back over my mother to hug her. To tell her that it's OK. That everything's going to be all right.

Then the curtains are suddenly drawn back and a doctor steps through. He ignores me.

'Good morning, Mrs Taylor, how are you feeling?'

He is tall and skinny, with a lot of red hair, and blue eyes.

Mum raises her head slightly from the pillow and answers, 'Doctor, I just lost my daughter. How the hell do you think I'm feeling?'

The doctor apologises for his stupidity, and begins to examine her. He's still ignoring me.

I stand up and walk out of the ward. I've got to find out what's going on. In the middle of the busy reception area, I try to stop someone. Nobody responds. My headache comes back, and I have to stand still. Everyone's rushing past me and shouting. It hurts my head! I stand in the middle of all these people and scream!

Nobody stops. Nobody listens. Nobody can hear me! I try to grab hold of someone, but my hand goes straight through! I can't touch them!

A man walks up to the coffee machine and

presses a button. It works. Oh my God, it works! There's only one possible explanation: I must be dead.

I walk out of the open door, into the street. I think it's raining. I can't really tell. I can't feel any water, but people are walking around with umbrellas, probably moaning about being wet and cold. I would give anything to feel the rain, to know that I'm alive. I walk out of the hospital grounds and hear a baby cry. I cry too. But nobody hears *me*.

I wander down the High Street and see my friends all crowded around a phone box. I was supposed to meet them today. I move closer. They're calling my number. I could tell them that there's no one there, but they won't hear me. I trail after them as they shop for over an hour. They don't seem to miss me. They all laugh and have a great time without me.

I go to my own funeral. It's nice, some of the things they say.

I leave, along with my mother, before they bury my body. I climb into the car over her, and she drives home.

She unlocks the door and we both walk in. She sits down and begins to cry. Loud sobs that wrench at my heart. I can't bear to cause her so much pain. I try to let her know I'm here. I try to move things, but I can't. In despair I try to send her a message. But I don't think she gets it. I stare at the bunch of flowers on the table, and at the framed picture I gave her just a few days ago. I wish I could pick it up, give it to her. She'd know it's from me. I try to concentrate on the picture. I once read a book where this kid could move things with the power of his mind. It's the only thing I can think of that might work. As I gaze at it the picture slowly moves towards Mum, but the strain becomes too great and I have to drop it. I look at her to see if she noticed. She did. She is staring at the picture with a look of horror on her face. Maybe she doesn't know it's me. She runs out of the house, leaving me sitting there.

In ghost stories, you never see things from the point of view of the ghost. They're always evil, trying to scare people. Maybe they're not. Maybe they're normal people like me, just trying to communicate. To say, 'It's all right, I haven't really gone. I love you.'

I hear the sound of a key in the lock. Mum's home. She's brought someone with her. Claire, she's brought Claire. According to Mum, Claire is psychic. Maybe I can talk through her!

They both come into the sitting room, and sit on the sofa. Then Claire begins chanting something. I feel wave after wave of dizziness wash over me, and I feel lighter and lighter. Mum calls out, 'Roxy, I love you baby,' and I try to say it back. Then I begin to float. I open my eyes to bright countryside, and I am happy.

'She's gone,' said Claire, opening her eyes. 'But she had a message for you. She said she loves you too.'

'Do you think she'll understand,' said Jade Taylor shakily, 'that I can't live with her looking over my shoulder?'

'Yes,' said Claire. 'I think she will.'

The Pantomime Girl

BY NAOMI DE BERKER

Amongst the fit, lithe bodies I felt out of place.
With the sweat pouring off my red face and my
eleven-stone body desperately trying to keep
up with the exercises, I knew it had been a
mistake to come.

My agent had told me about an audition for
the local pantomime, saying I was just what
they wanted. Glancing around me, I wasn't so
sure. Everyone else seemed to be six feet tall,

with long shapely legs, blue eyes and all uniformly blonde. With my short stature, mousy hair and stout body, I didn't have a chance.

Once the exercises were over, I hung about waiting for the results and stared enviously at the Nordic beauties as they nonchalantly strolled by, nibbling rice cakes and carrots. They're like rabbits, I thought bitchily, secretly yearning for the calorie-ridden Mars bar in my bag, but not daring to eat it in such a weight-conscious atmosphere.

Fidgeting, I got my book, *The Loved Ones*, out of my bag. Immersing myself in the happy-ever-after scenario of the hopelessly romantic story line, I managed to forget my self-consciousness and relax. I've always loved books that you just know are going to end cheerfully, with no unpleasant surprises, unlike real life. However, I've never really empathised with the heroines. They always seem so annoyingly perfect. Just like this lot.

Finally the results were read out. 'Will these people please stay behind for the second part of the audition,' barked a beefy-looking matron with a steely glare. I got up, ready to leave, knowing that my name would not be one of those called.

Suddenly I heard it. 'Pardon?!' I screeched, reeling with shock.

The woman looked up from the list. 'Amy Hugh, please will you stay for a minute.' My face must have revealed my blank surprise, as she kindly showed me a chair saying, 'You're through, dear.' The last name called, the others started to leave. Many murderous and sceptical glances were thrown my way as they filed out.

They were more astounded than I was that I had been picked.

In a daze I followed the instructions and found myself eventually on stage. The girl before me, though beautiful, had sung like a strangled chicken. My hopes rose, since whatever else I lacked, I did at least have a pleasant singing voice.

Hearing the notes of my piece start, the lyrics of the song took me over, and I performed the accompanying dance. My nerves settled as I went through the familiar steps. All too soon it was over, and once again I sat down to await the director's decision.

The next act seemed startlingly good after all the ones before. The slim and striking blonde girl's melodious voice rose above the chatter of the other people waiting, and her dance was amazingly beautiful and graceful. There was a silence when her music finished, and then a roar of applause. Never before had I seen anyone so good. Once again I knew I didn't have a chance.

After what seemed like a decade, the director came to announce who had won. Looking around me I sighed, knowing I had to go back to work in McDonald's on Monday. There was no way I would get the part.

As he read out my name, I gave a strangled squeak. I could hardly suppress my squeals of joy. Almost skipping, I went to find out when rehearsals started. The director, looking worn, smiled as I approached. 'Well done,' he said, 'I can't tell you how glad I was when you turned up. We were looking for a fat Mother Hubbard, and you'll save us a lot of padding. And your comical dancing was marvellous. How did you know this was a comedy part? No one else seemed to.'

A Breath of Fresh Air

BY ADAM SMITH

As he walked down the worn out cobbled path, he could feel his lungs choking with the dirtiness of the country air. He coughed and spluttered; but it was no use, the filthy feeling remained. He glanced about him, and seeing that no one was near, he reached into his jacket and pulled out a small, purple-coloured cylinder. After looking around once more, he quickly ripped off the metal cap and took a small, rationed gasp of the refreshingly clean air. The sealed cylinder back in his jacket, hidden from sight, Malcolm moved slowly on through the dark country lanes.

As he continued steadily along his usual route home, everything was happening as it should, as it had every evening for as many years as he could clearly remember. He passed his neighbour – an elderly man whom Malcolm had known ever since had had left home, twenty-something years ago. Courteously Malcolm waved, but as he did so he inadvertently knocked the cylinder out of his pocket. He couldn't believe it – he was always so careful when he had fresh air on him. It hit the ground, sending an echoing, metallic clang through all the surrounding alleyways; people were running at him from everywhere, diving and fighting with each other to get at that small cylinder lying there in the middle of the road. Even his elderly neighbour had thrown his walking aid to the floor and was joining in with the clamouring crowds.

Malcolm knew what he had to do. He left the desperate body of people behind him as he ran as hard as he could. He didn't know where he was going, or even how long he would carry on running. All he knew was that he had to get away from that crowd. Eventually he collapsed in a grassy field after what seemed like hours of running. He lay on his back panting, his chest rising and falling like the waves of the sea, as he drew in the filthy air.

After a short while he became aware of someone behind him. He had not realised that a car had pulled up close by, coughing out polluting fumes into the air. Someone had got out and was walking slowly and meaningfully towards him, his feet falling silently on the brownish grass. Malcolm glanced up and saw the man's eyes, whose glare said more to him than any words could. He had seen him drop that canister – he knew that Malcolm had access to air, fresh air!

'Get in,' said the stranger, gesturing to his dark car. 'You're coming with me.'

Malcolm didn't resist – he knew it would be pointless.

'Where are you taking me?' he asked, once he'd regained his composure.

'That's up to you,' responded another character, the driver, in a low, growling voice. 'You know what we want. Where can we get it?'

'I don't know what you mean! What do you

want?' Deep down Malcolm knew that it was no use pretending in this way, but still he continued in his attempted deception. 'Honestly, I don't know how I can help you. What do you want?'

Malcolm was suddenly and painfully made to realise the futility of his argument as the stranger pinned him to the side of the vehicle. In the same moment Malcolm also realised that his suspicions as to the identity of these people were right. They were from The Group!

'You didn't get that fresh air from The Group did you?' the man shouted.

'I did, I swear!'

'You're lying,' the stranger replied more calmly, easing his grasp on Malcolm's neck. 'So I'll ask you one more time; where did you get the fresh air?'

Everyone knew that fresh air from The Group was only ever found in red, branded cylinders. Similarly, everyone knew that The Group did not take kindly to people finding fresh air by any other means. After all, it was only by monopolising the market that The Group could insist on any terms of sale to whoever was able to afford it. It was generally known that The Group had complete control over all the leaders of the world and therefore, without exaggeration, a similar degree of control over all the major companies, businesses and organisations everywhere! They all wanted, needed, fresh air and The Group made sure that they could only buy it from them – they could charge anything they liked for it, anything at all.

But Malcolm had discovered an alternative,

affordable supply of fresh air – and that is what The Group must have found out. And anyone caught defying their unwritten rules, anyone buying fresh air from someone else, would be punished – everyone knew that. But once tasted, Malcolm would do anything to get some fresh air. It was like a potent drug – he could never again be satisfied with the dirty air that they were all subjected to.

'How dare you try to undermine The Group!' the stranger shouted, breaking the silence. 'How dare you—'

'But I haven't done anything wrong,' Malcolm insisted. 'I just—'

'Silence!' roared the stranger. 'The Group will not tolerate people like you trying to tear down the society we have created. You will soon learn that we are the only force in the world!' He exchanged a meaningful glance with the driver, who responded with a sinister nod of the head.

Gazing steadily at his victim, the stranger advanced slowly on Malcolm, his gloved hands stretching out towards Malcolm's neck. 'You won't be needing *any* air where you're going...'

The Foot Doctor

BY MÁIRE MACNEILL

Amy hurried through the swirling grey mist. 'I must be nearly there,' she thought. She was going to visit her Aunt Amber, whom her mother had described as 'a bit odd in her ways'. Amy wondered what it would be like to stay with an aunt she had never met, especially one who was an eccentric foot surgeon. 'Oh well,' she decided, 'there could be worse things.' However, the truth was, she would really rather be going anywhere than the town of Little Toofon. To distract herself, she went over her plans for the future: first a PhD in Biology at Cambridge, then a cure for cancer, after which she would retire, rich and famous, when…

Wham! She had walked straight into a lamppost. 'No,' she realised, dazed, 'not a lamppost. A signpost.' It said: TOOFON FLATS.

'Ah,' she thought. 'Aunt Amber's address.'

Amy stared up at the bleak building… and up… and up… As her eyes reached the top, there was a rumble of thunder and a flash of lightning which illuminated the block. Suddenly it started pouring with rain, so she hurriedly heaved her bag up the steps to the main door and ran her finger down the list of names by the intercom. Miss A. Smyth. 'That's her,' Amy muttered. 'The thirteenth flat on the thirteenth floor. Interesting. Today's Friday the 13th. Coincidence...' She pressed the button next to her aunt's name.

'Hello?' came a disembodied voice from the speaker.

'Hi. This is Amy.'

'Darling! Come right up!'

The main door swung open and Amy walked into a lobby painted blood red, with matching carpet. Sodden and dripping, she pressed the lift button. The lift banged and rattled as it slowly came down, down, down...

Bing! It arrived at last. Amy dragged her bag through its doors and pressed the button for floor thirteen. The lift started with a jolt, taking her up as slowly as it had come down.

Finally, Bing! The lift reached the thirteenth

floor and the doors opened. She stepped out and walked along the corridor to flat thirteen. The doorbell was a 3D cartoon of a foot which played a tinny, whiny version of *Jerusalem* when she pressed it.

And did those feet, in ancient times
Walk upon England's pastures green...

The door opened. Amy had expected to see a tall woman wearing a white laboratory coat. Instead she saw a short woman wearing a long black dress with only one foot peeping out from below.

'Hello Amy,' Aunt Amber said in a deep husky voice.

'You have a really unusual doorbell...' Amy blurted out before she stopped to think. 'And why do you only have one foot?'

'Oh, I had both my feet sawn off so that I could do research on them, but then I only had enough money to buy a metal foot for one leg… my left one. You can hardly tell it's metal, can you?' Aunt Amber boasted. 'But heavens! You're soaking! I'll show you to your room,' she said kindly, 'and then fetch you a dry towel.'

She disappeared to the other end of the hall while Amy sat in her room for what seemed like ages. After a bit she decided to explore the flat and find out about her aunt's work. I could learn a few things from Aunt Amber, she thought as she opened a door marked STUDY. It was dark inside and she was about to flick on the light, when Aunt Amber's hand gently stopped her.

'Uh, uh, uh!' teased Aunt Amber. 'You mustn't go in there. It's the only place where I can work undisturbed. Now, change into something dry and then we can have a chat.' She draped a towel around Amy's shoulders.

Amy changed and joined her aunt in the sitting room.

'Hello dear,' said Aunt Amber, pushing a bowl across to Amy. 'Have a jelly foot.'

'A what?' spluttered Amy.

'Oh, it's a little sweet, dear. You know, like jelly cola bottles. We foot doctors have them all the time. Trade joke.' She winked at Amy, who by then was feeling rather bewildered.

'Um... I think it's really brave that you've sacrificed your feet for science,' stammered Amy timidly.

Aunt Amber laughed throatily. 'It's nothing,' she said. 'In fact, I've persuaded a few of my visitors to do the same. But I've never experimented on children's feet... I was wondering... How would you like to donate yours?'

Her voice had become soft and her gaze hypnotic. Amy desperately tried to think of a polite way of refusing this offer.

'Uh... You're joking, aren't you?' she said weakly.

'Oh, of course,' exclaimed Aunt Amber. She directed her gaze away from Amy's face, 'Although it's a shame really... such pretty feet. She gave a tinkling laugh at her niece's shocked expression.

Amy decided to change the subject very quickly. 'So what's it like, being a foot doctor? I want to become one myself one day, you see,' she said brightly, to cover her growing sense of alarm.

'Oh wonderful,' said Aunt Amber, just as brightly. 'And you would make such a good one! It's a lovely job. Peace all day when you're not at the clinic. I love having visitors, though… oh dear, where are my manners? I need to prepare supper. Come with me.'

Amy followed her uneasily into the kitchen. There was no sign of any food.

'What's for supper?' she asked casually.

'A particularly unique brand of meat.' Her aunt gave her a penetrating look.

'Oh sorry,' Amy apologised. 'I'm a vegetarian.'

Her aunt had a strange glint in her eye.

'But my dear,' she said, her voice silky soft as she sharpened her knife, 'that doesn't matter at all.'

To Infinity and Beyond

BY TOM PRESTON

Hi there, Nigel Butts here (yes, I know it's an unfortunate name, but it only causes about seventeen laughs a day).

I'm going to tell you about my inspired Science Fair Project and the science fair itself, from which the headmaster will never recover.

We had never had a science fair before at our school, so this was a bit of an experiment for us (to put it mildly) and one which we will never repeat thanks to Richard Smodley and his attempt to show the effect of spraying hydrogen on to a Bunsen-burner flame.

I got the idea for my project from the programme we had watched a few weeks back about animals being blasted into space. It may sound a bit ambitious, and it was, but I decided to send my sister's hamster into the great beyond, using a home-made rocket which runs on diesel (don't worry, I made it a little mini crash helmet).

The rocket was a beautiful thing, not a primitive contraption made out of washing-up bottles and sticky tape like you might expect, but an awe-inspiring, shining vision of sophistication and power.

The main carapace was the product of several hours of diligent work. Made of aluminium, it shone like a full moon on a winter's night, its sweeping lines conjuring up images of the sleek body of a dolphin, perfectly streamlined. Her name was The Goddess, and she stood, monumental and proud, at over four feet tall, on long sharkfin legs, painted a blazing red.

The bulge of the rocket booster and the distinctive smell of diesel in the air gave the only hint of the potential power of this beast.

The cockpit of the shuttle was another masterpiece. There were obviously no controls, but I had made a miniature leather chair (I'm sure my mum won't miss the tiny square of material missing from the back of her sofa!) which looked out of the Plexiglas window, hopefully on to the deserted, lonely void of space.

It was a labour of love, and had lost me several friends, but it was worth it and nothing would stop me from winning first prize at that fair.

There was only one person who could terminate my chances of winning before they even got off the ground (no pun intended), and that was my arch-nemesis, Trevor Barnsley. He was my ex-best friend (we had gone our separate ways after he stole my first and only love Mary Wilkinson and I threw custard over his head at lunch time) and would do anything to go one better than me.

Trevor's experiment was the teacher's favourite. It was based on the idea that listening to the sound of crickets chirping improves the standard of a pupil's work. Instead of using a recording, he had used real crickets, kept in a glass tank – so *his* project was open to sabotage (evil laugh).

After I had completed my rocket, the only thing left for me to do was train my sister's hamster to cope with the rigours of this journey into the unknown.

My initial worry was whether it could withstand the immense pressures of space flight, so I built a simulator based on the ones real astronauts use at NASA. I made a pivot for the main arm out of a wedge-shaped piece of wood, with a plywood base, which was bolted to the floor. On top of this, attached by a four-inch nail to the top of the pivot, I placed a long arm (about three feet) made from an old piece of copper pipe we had in the garage.

At one end of this arm was a weight equal to the mass of the hamster, and at the other end was a clear plastic bubble, made from one of those detergent containers which go in the washing machine. The hamster (sorry, astronaut) was placed in this bubble, and the arm was spun around by hand, as fast as I could make it go. (I can still hear the whuush of that simulator on quiet nights even now. Ah, happy memories.) This would simulate the rocket's take-off. The rest of the training was watching the video of *Apollo 13* (a very appropriate film).

The day of the science fair finally arrived, and it was by no means an anticlimax. The sun was beaming merrily away, the birds were twittering in the trees, and we came to school in high spirits, excited at the prospect of showing off our scientific genius. It seemed as if nothing could possibly go wrong.

The morning was spent setting up our experiments and making derogatory comments about each other's work. The fair was to be held in the main hall, and I set my rocket up underneath an open skylight, so it would have an unimpeded take-off (in theory).

The only event worth recording was when Trevor's crickets escaped from their glass case and caused our big, tough PE teacher, Mr Hurton, to run out of the room shrieking like a girl when one of them landed on his head (I wonder how that happened? Evil laugh).

After lunch, it was time for the teachers to see the results of our hard work.

Michael Flatley's diorama was the first to be judged. It was made out of Plasticine and showed a very unflattering model of our science teacher taking a chemistry class. Not surprisingly, it wasn't very well received.

Next came Maria Water's models of different types of housing, ranging from straw huts to the very latest developments (her dad is an architect).

From then on it started to go downhill when, with much trepidation, the judges looked at Richard Smodley's effort, the aforementioned Bunsen-burner experiment. This was as dangerous as it sounds and resulted in a medium-sized fireball engulfing Maria's display, setting her precious row of houses alight. The headmaster rushed to the scene with a fire extinguisher, but by the time the fire had been put out, both of the displays were ruined.

If I could make my rocket work, it looked as

if I had it in the bag (as Trevor – sadly – never found his crickets).

I started off with a short explanation of what I wanted to do, fended off a few questions about the safety of the hamster, and got straight down to business.

I instructed everyone to stand back, and lit the fuse. They watched with bated breath as the spark spat and spluttered slowly towards the engine. There were gasps of wonderment as the fuel ignited and the rocket rose majestically towards the heavens… and hit the ceiling. It had veered off course, and its maiden voyage ended in a small explosion, the tiny form of the hamster drifting down on its home-made parachute. (Luckily, I had foreseen this eventuality.)

This was the final nail in the coffin of the

science fair, and a decision was taken never to hold another one.

The day ended with the headmaster apologising to the parents for such a catastrophic series of events. Even this was marred when my sister's hamster (which had somehow escaped) decided to nibble at the headmaster's shoes in revenge for the way he'd been treated. This was a source of great hilarity for the parents, who had thoroughly enjoyed the entire fiasco.

As for my beautiful rocket, all that was left was a little brass plaque reading: TO INFINITY AND BEYOND.

The Kiss

BY HOLLIE PRITCHARD

The new metal world clinked and clanked,
social and love lives taken over by holograms.
Your turn to have a baby? Take a form from the
chemist and tick the pink box for a girl or the
blue box for a boy, next day delivery, available
for just £2000. Giving birth in the natural way
ended around the year 2050. Even kissing and
touching are now forbidden due to the
outbreak, the escape of the virus that was

supposed to have been secretly contained under scientific eyes two centuries ago. Now if you want any sort of intimate relationship you have to use interactive fantasy devices with a holographic boyfriend or girlfriend.

It is the year 2106 and there is no naturalistic environment to be seen. All the luscious green trees, planted by ancestors, have been hacked down by the world's latest mechanical machine invention, and have been replaced by yet another pristine metal building: ugly and shapeless. Neon lights give the air an artificial quality.

In this New World, if you are poor and underprivileged, you might as well forget life: you don't count for anything, you're just overlooked. If you are born into this state, you haven't got a hope in hell.

Listen To Me!

As Zelda ambled along the barren alley, her clothes ragged and torn, she counted the euros which lay on her palm, which was sandpaper-coarse. There were only three. Not enough for a couple of meal-making pills, or even one for that matter.

A man called from the end of the alley. His face was half hidden in the shadows but, from what Zelda could see, he had a well-chiselled figure. As she drew nearer she could see that he was a well-dressed and extravagant-looking young man, ripe at the age of about nineteen.

She wished to save herself from the humiliation of being seen in her shabby rags by such an imposing specimen of the male species, so she cloaked herself within the shadows and waited until she was sure that the young man had gone.

The Kiss

One week passed and Zelda still couldn't help thinking about the man from the alley – his olive skin, dark hair and masculine body, she could just picture it…

But her daydream came to an abrupt end when the noise of sirens filled the air.

Zelda got this feeling every time someone looked at her – usually in open disapproval. She turned round to confront the observer only to find it was the man from the alley, but to her surprise his eyes were filled with pity rather than disgust.

As he looked beyond the rags he saw something which was rare to him – real beauty. Her naturally jet-black hair coiled in ringlets around her delicate face; her lips were full but not with the help of any cosmetic surgery procedure; and her complexion was clear and without artifice.

When he could see through his forbidden thoughts he managed, hesitantly, to ask Zelda who she was. She spoke in a somewhat reluctant and timid voice.

'Zelda, my name is Zelda. What is yours?' The man seemed overjoyed that she had spoken to him. He replied, 'My name's Jack Binxon, but you can call me Binx.' He paused for a moment and then said in a slightly embarrassed voice, 'You look freezing. Why don't you come back to my apartment to get warm and have some meal-making tablets?'

Something clicked with Zelda; have a meal-making pill, and get warmed up at my place? It was really just a chance for some quick cyber sex. Zelda's face changed from a grateful to a disgusted look. She looked at him, her face showing some uncertainty, and blurted out, 'You think just because I haven't got no money or decent clothes, I'm meaningless or easy!'

'No I wasn't implying that, honest,' Binx said in a raging, yet soothing tone. 'I just thought that you might be grateful for something to eat and a warm place to stay for an hour or so.'

Zelda looked at him. It would seem that he was telling the truth.

Binx's house was filled with the latest technology. He even had a holographic TV, which allowed you to see anyone you wanted, in holographic form, in your living room.

Binx and Zelda occupied themselves with talking about their pasts. Binx only had a mum left, but he hadn't seen her in two years. He just supposed she was too busy to get in touch, although it wouldn't have taken her two minutes to zap a hologram through to him, would it? His dad died of the virus when Binx was just five, and so had most of his other relations as well.

None of Zelda's family was left. Her mother died of the virus when she was seven. She did have a dog, but it got crushed under a landing hovercraft. Zelda was very lonely. Any money she earned was from the few people that took pity on her and threw her a few euros.

Time was quickly passing and Zelda was getting used to the warmth of the computerised heating system. But things just didn't seem right. Why was Binx being so nice? Zelda looked at Binx with a puzzled expression on her face.

It was then Binx knew that he had found love. He drew his masculine body closer to hers until Zelda could feel his breath condensing on her neck and she became very nervous.

'If we get caught we'll be dead, there's no doubt about it,' Zelda spoke with extreme anxiety. Binx had a thoughtful look on his face, and after a short pause, he answered, 'No one will ever know.'

At precisely the same moment, they were both filled with a lust for the real thing, not just the fake buzz that you'd get from an interactive fantasy device.

Almost immediately, the forbidden lust overtook them and their lips touched in an unlawful kiss. For that one instant of pleasure, they knew they would suffer a lifetime of misery.

Through the window, the hovercraft drifted into view; it was the police.

Dragon Problems

BY ALVIN SHUM

Cecil the knight stared at the opening of the
cave. A small constant wisp of smoke could be
seen coming out of the entrance. He crept in.
There was the dragon! Asleep on a rock and
snoring. He drew his sword out of its scabbard
and moved up to the dragon. Unfortunately the
beast had very good hearing and heard Cecil
step on a twig. The dragon opened up an eye,
searching the cave for any unwanted guests.

'Who's there?' he asked as he rose up.

'Spawn of the devil, prepare to meet thy doom,' stammered Cecil.

'Oh no,' groaned the dragon. 'It's a knight. Can't you read the sign outside the cave?'

'What sign?' enquired Cecil, who was rather surprised by this reaction.

'Look at this,' said the dragon, and he walked out of the cave and pointed at a brass sign.

```
CAVE OF DRAGON
PRIVATE PROPERTY!
IF KNIGHT OR TOURIST,
DO NOT ENTER.
YOU HAVE BEEN WARNED!
```

'See, you're entering private property,' said the

dragon. 'I'm now obliged to sue you.'

'Sue! What do you mean, sue? I came here for a fight, and I'm going to get one,' retaliated the knight.

'What do I get out of it?'

'Pardon?' asked the knight.

'I said, what do I get out of it? I mean, if I die you get all the treasures in the cave and, no doubt, half of the kingdom and the king's daughter's hand in marriage.'

'You don't get anything out of it, you're a dragon.'

'Are you Christian?' asked the dragon.

'Of course I am,' replied Cecil. 'All knights are Christian.'

'Well, you can't kill me then,' said the dragon. 'Remember the Book of *Exodus*: thou shalt not kill?'

'But you're not human!' cried out Cecil.

'Now that's what I call racist,' said the dragon. 'Just because I'm fifty feet high, breathe fire, eat the occasional cow and roast a few buildings, I have to be killed. I mean, what about my family? Don't they get any compensation?'

'I don't see any children or wife.'

'We're divorced,' sobbed the dragon. 'She gets the dragonets one decade and I get them the next decade.'

'I'm sorry. I'm just a knight: I kill any rampaging monsters, free maidens once in a while – that sort of thing,' said Cecil.

'Well, I don't see any rampaging monsters around here, do you?'

'No,' admitted Cecil.

'My mother warned me against marrying

her. She said she was only marrying me for my gold. I suppose she's right.' The dragon began crying again.

Cecil began to feel guilty. He was never taught to be a psychologist when he was training to become a knight. He shuffled to his feet.

'Now you're going to kill me as well,' cried out the dragon.

'Well, what if I don't kill you? How about that then, hmm? Sounds fair to me,' said Cecil. It was the only thing he could think of to say.

'Really?' stammered the dragon. 'That would be really nice. I mean, if you promise not to kill me, then I won't burn any more villages or hurt anyone.'

'What about the cattle?' asked Cecil.

'You expect me to starve?' snapped the

dragon. 'Do I look like a vegetarian?'

'Sorry,' said Cecil. 'I didn't mean to be rude.'

'Don't worry about it,' said the dragon. 'It's awfully nice of you to let me go free. I'm useless at fighting. Got bullied by my brothers.'

'Well, goodbye then,' said Cecil.

'Cheerio,' said the dragon. 'If you need any help, you know where I am.

And, as they say in the best fairy stories, they all lived happily ever after. Cecil got on his horse and rode away back to the castle. He informed the king that he had killed the dragon and, as his reward, received half the kingdom, and the hand of the princess in marriage.

The dragon's divorce settlement was agreed upon shortly afterwards, and he soon met another dragon with whom he immediately fell in love.

Prince Cecil soon became King Cecil, and lived a long and prosperous life. He never fought against another soul and certainly never told anybody about his strange encounter with the dragon suffering a mid-life crisis.

How Love First Came to Be

BY FARIHA SHAIKH

My grandchild, my grandchild, come, sit round the glowing embers of this fire and I shall tell you a story. When you are old, you shall tell this story to your children and your children's children. They will tell theirs, and so the story will be passed down through the generations. Core of my heart, listen carefully, and learn...

Once, long ago, when the ticking of time had only just begun, there were two tribes.

They were always arguing about everything, with each other, and even within each tribe.

It is sad, little one, so sad, the way they argued and fought endlessly. Petty squabbling that escalated eventually into war. And when the two tribes grew tired of this, they signed peace treaties, but even then, their arguments did not cease.

One day, during a skirmish, somebody killed a member of the other tribe. Intentionally or accidentally, we do not know. And I suppose, my grandson, it doesn't matter because either way, it would not have stopped the war the two sides were now ready for. What a long and bloody war it was. So many lives lost for ever, so many lives.

My grandchild, you must know that real hatred possessed the minds of these men so that they wanted to kill as many men as they could of the other tribe before they were killed themselves.

Then came the awful day when most of the men were killed. It was a dreadful time. The two sides fought long and hard. Towards evening, under the darkening sky, the field that had once held beautiful flowers now held disfigured bodies. Bodies of the dead and dying. The air was full of the moans of pain and anguish. But the living took no notice, for as they stood, the great Sun God slipped over their heads. Towards the sea he went, my dearest, towards that cool bed of water. And the two tribes watched in awe.

They had never seen the Sun God so close before. Then a great miracle happened. The moon, sister to the great Sun God, appeared.

Have you ever seen the moon rise with the sun? No, you have not, for it is not permitted for Sister Moon to catch up with the great Sun God.

The great Sun God spoke, my son, but not in the way that humans speak. He said, 'You,' and pointed one long fiery arm at the two tribes. His voice was so full of sorrow. Sorrow at having to watch two tribes fight for so long, two tribes that could have been one.

'If it was my desire, I could burn you all out of existence! But, out of mercy, I will not. My Sister Moon and I will give you one more chance. ONE MORE CHANCE!'

He spoke with a voice that seemed to come from all directions. A voice that seemed to fill the heavens, the sea and the space between them, until it reached all the corners of the

Listen To Me!

Earth and thundered in the ears of men. And then he went down, below the foamy waves, leaving the moon to rise and spread her hair over the sky for the shiny stars to twinkle on it. Then she spoke.

In a voice as gentle as a brook tumbling over stones, water chasing water, laughing, singing, Sister Moon said, 'I tell you to stop this killing, and you will stop. So much blood need not be shed; so many souls need not be lost.

'I will give you a box, and tell you where to keep it. What I will not tell you is what is in the box. That you must find out for yourselves. After seven days and seven nights, you may open it. You must spread its contents all over the Earth. After that, you will not fight and you will never again open the box. For if you do, great woe will fall upon you all.

'People, you must learn to be one nation, you must learn to live peacefully, to think before you act, but, above all, you must learn to love.'

As she spoke, her words echoed again and again from the hills to the sea.

Well, my grandson, this tale draws to its end as all tales do.

The people did as they were told. The fighting stopped, but the tribes still did not speak to each other. The elder ones took heed of Sister Moon. They listened to her and remembered her words with fear. They opened the box when the time came. And in it, my love, they found some dust, not the ordinary dust that collects on the floor of our huts, no, for this dust was mist blue in colour. They knew at once that it did not come from anywhere on this earth...

The two tribes looked at one another, wondering how to carry out the task the Moon had set them. They realised they would have to discuss this matter with each other.

And this, my grandson, was the first time they had talked to each other without using harsh and cruel words. As they sprinkled the dust over the land, they felt a warmth within them. One man talked to another from the same tribe, smiling. One woman talked to another from a different tribe. For the first time since the world had been created there was a feeling of love. It was as if their hearts had been made of stone but now at last the stone had been replaced by real flesh and warm blood.

How Love First Came to Be

And the places that the dust did not touch, child, these are the dark places of the Earth, where murders are committed. These are the places that love did not reach…

So that is the end of my story. Of how love came to abound on Earth and how the heavenly bodies united two tribes and taught them love and respect.

Fool's Gold

BY STEPHEN HUMPHREY

King Henry the Eighth and his Royal Advisor stood at the dockside, watching the *Mary Rose* sink.

'I suppose that's going to be expensive?' King Henry asked, scratching the back of his neck anxiously, watching as all the little sailors swam out of the fast-disappearing vessel.

'VERY expensive, Your Majesty,' the Advisor said. 'Do you know how much money we spent on that ship?'

'No, but don't worry, we can easily afford it,' Henry said, coolly.

'No we can't,' the Advisor sighed. 'We're broke.'

'Broke? What, me?!' Henry asked, in disbelief.

The Advisor nodded.

'But… but how can this be? I'm the King, for goodness' sake! Never before has a king experienced financial difficulties!'

'Yes, but you're the first king to have six square meals a day, Your Majesty,' the Advisor said.

Back at the palace, Henry was eating a pheasant with one hand and holding the royal savings in the other.

'That's it?' he roared.

'That is all, yes, sire,' the Bursar nodded.

'I see,' Henry grunted. Then after a pause, he announced, 'What we need, Bursar, is a plan.'

'I've got an idea!' shouted the Advisor, running into the dining hall.

'Careful, man, you almost made the waiter drop the roast duck! Who told you to stop? Come on, I've almost finished my fourth course already!' Henry shouted to the waiter standing sheepishly in the doorway. 'Now, have you come up with a plan yet?'

'We need an alchemist!' the Advisor said.

'A what?' the Bursar asked.

'An alchemist experiments with metals to try and turn them into gold,' the Advisor explained. 'We'll find the best alchemist in

England, and soon we'll be rolling in gold!'

Out on the heathlands, there was a loud bang, and all the birds flew away. That was Thomas Mariner's first explosion of the day. And his third hut that week.

Thomas Mariner was the country's only alchemist. And its worst. So far in his career, he'd ruined thirty huts, fifty-eight suits of clothes, killed twenty-two birds and burnt down six trees. And he'd only taken up alchemy six months ago.

That morning, a horse and cart came rolling across the heath, containing two of the King's guards and a distinguished-looking gentleman. This, Thomas decided, could either be very good news, or very bad news. He was, however, an optimist by nature. Alchemists have to be.

'Are you Thomas Mariner?' the gentleman asked, sounding a little anxious.

'Yes, sir. What may I do for you?' Thomas replied.

'I am a messenger from King Henry the Eighth. At present, the palace is experiencing slight, erm, financial trouble. Therefore, His Majesty wishes you to make him some gold,' the Advisor explained. 'Will you come?'

'Work for the King? Thank you, but I'd rather not…' Thomas said. 'Too much pressure…'

'I see,' the Advisor replied, nodding to a guard. The guard stepped forward and knocked Thomas out. 'Sorry, but you have no choice. And neither have we,' the Advisor added.

Thomas regained consciousness inside a dark, cold room. He wasn't sure where he was, but he decided that it was probably bad.

'Mr Mariner! Welcome to the palace!' said a jovial voice. 'I understand you didn't want to come and work for me.'

Thomas realised it was the King.

'S...sorry, Your Majesty. But the pressure is so great...' he stammered.

'Pressure? No, there's no pressure. I just want lots of gold and I want it by tomorrow morning, OK? Now, this is your little workshop. It's time for my fifth meal of the day, so I'm going to leave you to it. Oh, and Mariner...'

'Yes?'

'Fail me, and you're dead.'

'Are you sure he's the best?' Henry asked, trying to eat a whole roast lamb in one mouthful.

'He's all there is, Your Majesty, unless of course you want to look abroad,' the Advisor said.

'Oh no, we don't want a foreigner. I suppose we'll have to stick with Mariner. After all, it's not as though…'

King Henry's next words were drowned out by an almighty explosion. The entire palace shook and a chandelier fell from the ceiling, landing in the sherry trifle.

After a few minutes, a large pile of rubble shifted as Henry got up. The Advisor also struggled out, surveying the mess and devastation.

'I don't believe it!' Henry roared. 'This is an outrage! That blasted alchemist has ruined my trifle! MARINER!'

Thomas ran up a flight of stairs, which

collapsed behind him.

'Ooops?' he said, sounding hopeful.

'You have one last chance,' Henry said, smouldering quietly. 'If you do not make me some gold by tomorrow morning, I'll have you beheaded faster than Anne Boleyn!'

'Thomas Mariner, Royal Alchemist,' the guard announced the following morning.

'Come in, man, come in! Have you made me some gold?' Henry asked.

Thomas gulped, nervously. 'I... have, Your Majesty,' he nodded.

'What?' King Henry, the Advisor and the Bursar asked, all at the same time.

'You mean you've actually made gold? You?' Henry asked.

'Yes, Your Majesty. And here it is,' Thomas

said, placing a shining piece of gold before Henry's throne.

'That can't be gold. He couldn't make a cake, let alone gold!' the Advisor said in disbelief.

'Advisor, I advise you to shut up,' Henry said, eyeing up the gold excitedly. 'This is it! We can pay for the *Mary Rose* and still have plenty besides! Mariner, you are free to go!'

'Erm, don't I get a reward or something?' Thomas asked hopefully.

'A reward?' Henry said. 'Oh, well… here, have this,' and he threw Thomas a roast peacock. 'Enjoy it, if you know how to.'

The Advisor stopped Thomas as he was leaving the palace.

'All right, alchemist,' he said. 'You may have

pulled the wool over Henry's eyes, but not mine. How did you really make that gold?'

'It was easy really,' Thomas said. 'That gold is just a rock covered in bronze. It's fake. Fool's gold, Advisor. Just right for King Henry. Now, can you show me how to eat a peacock?'

I am Ninety-Nine

BY OLIVER DIMSDALE

I am ninety-nine. When I was born, Queen Victoria was still on the throne; there had been no world wars; Britain was at war with the Boers in South Africa – all of which is now consigned to history lessons.

Since I was born, the world has changed: radio, television, aeroplanes, decimalisation, computers – I preceded all of these.

As the world has changed, so have I. When

I was a child, I thought as a child should, unaware of events in the outside world. As a banker, I thought as a banker should, my mind on money, intent on doing a good job. As a husband, I thought as a husband, caring and loving. As a father, I thought as a father, protective and concerned.

Now I am a great-grandfather, and I am considered too unimportant to have an independent voice. I find that I am an embarrassment, something to shut away and never be talked about.

As I have grown older, it seems that I have become a child again. I am no longer able to make decisions for myself. I am not allowed to live on my own, lest I should accidentally kill myself.

However, from the way my so-supportive

family behave whenever I want to see them, it seems that they would rather that I did die. Apparently, the only reason I am useful is my will. My possessions don't hold any sentimental value. The family merely wishes to sell them and take the money. It is ironic that when I die, I will only be useful for money – the commodity that I spent the best part of my life working with. It almost seems like poetic justice that I have become what I despised when I was younger: an elderly embarrassment with little time to live.

I am a friend. A friend to whom? Everyone who was my friend is long dead. Who should I talk to? Graves? I am not so far into senility that I find it necessary to talk to inanimate objects. My family would say that I am in a home so I can socialise with people my own age. Words reserved for children. It is impossible to find intelligent conversation with those mindless vegetables. conversations about who has died recently; what they used to do; the weather.

I feel betrayed, and now regret my feelings towards my own elderly relatives. I fought to protect this country, I could have died saving this country; I raised my children, my grandchildren. I am repaid with a room in a retirement home. I am forced to live amongst vegetables, because these vegetables do not see me as others see me. I am supposed to be elderly, and yet I am treated as a child. The nurses, my family: full of patronising phrases, nanny-like ways. If I ever complain, I only receive yet more patronising remarks. I hate these people, as much as I hated the patronising teachers at the school I attended. Nobody listened to me then, either.

I am a lonely, sad old man. When I think of my life, nothing was ever as bad as this. During the war, at least we had each other. Nothing compares to the intense isolation I feel. Even when people talk to me, they are not listening to my replies. In the past I was admired, my opinions valued, my family cared about me. I was working with intelligent people, earning a steady wage – a wage larger than most. With this I was able to provide generously for my family. I gave so much to my children, but now they barely recognise me – yet they are no longer young themselves. It is difficult for me to realise that these are the same people whom I raised from birth, helped through their education, whose children I supervised when they had other things to do. Rather than me losing my mind, it is they who seem to be forgetting everything they ever knew. Without my presence, their lives would have been so different, and now, how do they thank me? Collecting me once a year at Christmas. I can imagine their voices after I have left: 'Thank goodness he's gone.' 'That's it for another year.' 'I hope we never see him again.'

I feel angry that I – who was once so happy, possessing everything I wanted – am now reduced to a condition where I envy a sponge beneath the sea. Even this is not an adequate comparison: even a sponge beneath the sea has a more contented life than I.

I am so lonely. My only companion is the television. Even that is not ideal; there is so much offal broadcast these days. Most of it seems to be designed for either children or the mindless vegetables whom I despise. I know I am old, but I still have my mind. Everything seems to have changed. There are far too many homosexuals on television, and they seem to be encouraged. The women are no better. They wear skirts that hardly cover their backsides, and have exposed arms and the youth of the present day has only these for their role models.

I have spoken of this to my great-grandchildren many times, but nobody listens – nobody cares. I can sense their feelings: 'Here he goes again.' They do not treat me with the respect that my age commands. I feel that I should have respect. None of them would be around but for me.

But now I come to think about it, I was the

same when I was their age. I never realised the pain that is caused by being totally ignored. I am confused. I am supposed to be suffering the final stages of senile decay. I am supposed to prefer my own company. I am supposed to be disapproving, deaf and incontinent. I am supposed to constantly be talking about the past.

But the truth is, I am ninety-nine and unwanted.

The Start of the World as we Know It

BY PHILIP REID

God made the World and the World was round. (Actually it was roundish with bumps, but that doesn't sound as good.) God said, 'Let there be light,' and his angels fumbled with the light switch and there was light. He called the light 'day' and the darkness 'night'.

The next day, God got up. After eating his holy Coco Pops (without milk, because he hadn't made cows yet), he took blue spray paint and sprayed the sky, but he ran out so he left some white bits. These white bits were where the sky's plaster showed through. Gradually, they turned grey and leaked. Most of these grey leaking bits were placed over England (soon to be completed). Then God got an extra-large-multi-family-box of Plasticine and rolled it into a ball. He added bits of different coloured Plasticine on the blue stuff: there was white at the top and bottom, but the rest was mostly green stuff. God got a plastic modelling knife (so he wouldn't cut himself), and fiddled around with the green stuff. Small flicks of his knife created huge cliffs; little pushes left gaping holes; gentle scrapings made deep river beds. Twice, the knife slipped, resulting in the Grand Canyon and Mount Everest. Then it was getting dark, so God had to go to bed.

The next morning, God got up early. It was still quite dark so he got a 10,000 watt light bulb from the hardware store. Then, after carefully switching the electricity off so he didn't electrocute himself, God put the light bulb in its socket, so that he could always have light during the day. After he did this God thought, 'I cannot leave my light on all the time. I will need something else, so that I can see at night.' As he was thinking this, he was absentmindedly chucking the World up in the air, when a continent came off. God read the name he had conveniently put on all the lands. This one said 'Moon'. He tried to stick it on again, but the place where it went was messed up. God chucked 'Moon' up in the air (his pet habit), and it stuck on the ceiling. God really couldn't be bothered to get it down, so he left it up there where it reflected the bulb's light.

God wasn't sure what to do next, so he bought a book called *So You Want to Make Your Own World?* (not including instructions for Heaven and Hell). He started reading it and got up to 'Making Decorations – It's Easy!', when his mum called him up to bed. He slept with the book under his pillow.

The next day, God got up early again. He sprinkled the packet of 'Quick Grow' seeds, that came free with his book, over the Plasticine. Trees and plants sprang up all over the World, and it looked much better. The seeds made poppies, oaks and daisies. They made seaweed and algae, in the oceans. As God was clumsy (Remember Mount Everest?) some places – the rain forests - had too much vegetation. Some – the deserts - none at all.

After God had made the trees and plants, he breathed on the World. Then all the Plasticine became real, bursting with life and movement. As the World was only the size of his head, God took a magnifying glass and looked at it. It was fascinating. God watched for two hours (or 271 earth days) and saw the planted seeds grow and pollinate and spread over the evolving, growing World. After so much concentrated watching, God had a headache, so he took a pill and went to bed.

The next day, God set to work on animals to inhabit his world. He started small, with beetles and other insects. He made two of each, a male and a female. He then worked his way up to larger animals, the elephant and the giraffe. Then he made the sea animals, the little plankton, the playful dolphin and the whale. He made the predators – sharks, tigers and hawks. Two of each species. He put them on his living world and breathed on them, until they too were living. Then God went to bed.

The next morning, God had his cereal *with* milk, and his toast with butter and honey. He went to look at the earth and he liked what he saw. But he felt something was missing. So God took the last of the Plasticine, and made a man. It took ages. He put in every last detail – every hair, every inch of skin was perfect. It was his best ever creation. But he couldn't think what to call the man. After looking in his name dictionary he wavered between Adam and Wallace. He went for Adam because it was shorter. Then he breathed on Adam, and Adam became alive. But Adam was lonely, so God made a companion for him. After deciding not to call the companion Gromit (it sounded like a dog) he chose the name Eve, because it was also short. He put Adam and Eve on the earth and everything was complete.

The following day, God got up at eleven o' clock and didn't know what to do. So he just shouted at the cherubs and relaxed.

And that was the first week.

The Apprentice

BY ELIZA CHAN

Nervously, Pete pushed the oak door open and slipped into the hall. The room was a massive forest. The walls were made of tree trunks, intertwined so that there was not a single chink in the smooth wooden expanse. Looking up, Pete could see the hanging branches of the trees that formed a roof with their clasped fingers of leaves. He could feel the warmth of the sunlight fall on his face as the leaves swayed gently in the breeze. He held his hands up to the roof in silent joy at the sight before him.

A single leaf fell from the treetops and spiralled lazily down until it landed in Pete's eager hands. He touched the precious, five-cornered leaf with a delicate finger as he stared at it enchantedly.

'Are you quite finished, boy?' a quietly amused voice asked.

Startled, Pete looked up and suddenly remembered why he was here. He moved forward quickly and bowed his head in shame before the Grand Magician. He saw an old man before him with long silver hair and sparkling green eyes. The man scrutinised Pete critically as he arched one of his eyebrows.

'Such a slight thing, and yet she has

chosen…' he murmured to himself.

'Sir?' asked Pete in confusion.

'Oh yes, the test,' the old magician said, with plain annoyance in his voice. He cracked his knuckles and then leaned forward in his seat so that he was at eyelevel with Pete.

'What would you give to be a magician?'

Pete knew the question was coming. He had spoken to the other boys who had been tested before him, as they all waited outside the magician's castle nervously. Some had said they would give up their family and friends; others said they would give up riches and even their own freedom. Pete thought about the question carefully. He could not bear to give up his mother, who was his only relation in the world. She loved him dearly, and as much as he wanted to learn the art of magic, he was not willing to sacrifice her.

Then he thought about all his material goods: his dog and his flute. His dog had a mind of her own and did not really belong to him. Furthermore, he felt that if he gave up his flute, he would be lying. Pete was skilled with his fingers and could make a new flute in days. He knew that he would not miss his present flute much, so this did not really seem fair.

As much as he tried to think about it, Pete could not think of a single thing that he truly owned and that he could do without. Desperate for something to say, he replied: 'Myself, and only myself – for I am the only thing in this world that I have the right to sacrifice.'

The magician looked pleased at this answer. He beckoned the boy closer and whispered in his ear. 'I have chosen you; *you* are to be my new apprentice…'

'But I have not sat any test…'

'That was your test. Not everybody has the courage to look deep into themselves and admit that they own nothing except themselves; that nothing matters except their own minds. Besides, Loudara chose you.'

'Loudara? Who is Loudara?'

'Loudara is the presence in this room. She is the stem of all magic, the root of our past. Loudara is this!' he exclaimed as he rested his palm on the oaken walls of the room.

Hesitantly, Pete looked at the leaf that had fallen into his hands. It seemed to glow as it accepted him as its follower. A faint voice echoed through his mind. It whispered like stars on a cloudy night, so distant and unclear, yet so beautiful. Pete placed his hand beside the magician's on the wall. He could feel Loudara rippling through his mind and dancing joyfully through his heart. She whispered a name that seemed to awaken his inner eye and soul, yet was not familiar to his outer core.

He pulled his hand away from the wood in quiet fear. It was all too much too soon. He was only a peasant boy, yet now Loudara was saying that his destiny was to be…

'She is showing you too much, boy. Do not worry, she is impatient because I do not have the enthusiasm of youth that I once did!' the magician comforted Pete lightly.

Then he boomed, 'Your first lesson will be tomorrow at dawn. Please bring a bag with you to carry all your books in – please don't interrupt – where was I? Oh yes, at the end of your first year you will be allowed to come on an expedition with me— I said please don't interrupt, boy! What is it? It had better be important!'

'Please sir, I… I can't read or write.'

The magician guffawed loudly until he realised that the boy was not joking. As his laughter died away through the hall, he brought out a large book from a hidden cavity in the wall and began to write with a quill pen as he read his words aloud. 'Loudara chose my apprentice, a small boy with dark hair and a pleasant face. Unfortunately he believes he cannot write—'

'But I can't write!' interrupted Pete.

The magician continued without comment. 'His name is…'

He stopped writing and handed the book to Pete. Then he handed the boy the quill. Pete looked up in obvious anxiety. Didn't the magician realise that he meant what he said?

Unwilling to admit his ignorance a third time, Pete frowned and placed his quill to paper. Instinctively, his hand moved across the parchment, copying the loops and curves of the magician's writing. He could hear Loudara in his ear again, whispering the same word over and over like a chant.

Satisfied with what he had written, although he had no idea what it said, Pete handed the quill and book back to the old man. The Grand Magician studied what Pete had written with great interest. He looked up at the boy and extended his staff to him. 'And so you are one of us. You will be known hereafter as *Merlin*.'

Then Merlin suddenly realised who he was.

The Apprentice

He understood his role in history and accepted it. 'It shall be as you wish, Loudara,' he whispered. 'I will obey what is written. I am Merlin.'

Valentine Disaster

BY MARC DODI

Tuesday 14th February

Today is the day that I began my investigation with my associate, Bill. He's not the most reliable person in the world, but he'll do.

The day began like any other. I walked to school completely oblivious to the atmosphere around me. For today, you see, was Valentine's Day and I'd forgotten. When I actually got to school it became very clear to me that it was

Valentine Disaster

Valentine's Day. Why? Because there was a great big Valentine banner draped over the front gate.

In class everybody was giving out cards apart from me. When I got to my desk there was a card decorated with pink and red bows. My face was sweating all over. Who would send me a Valentine card? I opened it slowly and curiously. It said:

To Michael,
Be my Valentine and I will lavish flowers on you.
My sincerest love,

??

I had a secret admirer!

The whole day was a blur. My mind was fixed on who had sent the card. When I got home I went straight to my bedroom and thought it over. I thought for hours and hours, trying to imagine who could have written it. I had three suspects:

1. **Betsy Formal**: A really ugly and hideous girl who drools whenever she looks at me or at any other boy. DISGUSTING!
2. **Catrina de Ball**: Quite nice, but not much on her. Only that she sits next to me.
3. **Wendy Soh**: Not much on her either – except she has a pet hamster called Michael.

After that I kind of fell asleep, not doing a single piece of homework.

* * *

Wednesday 15th February

At 7:30 a.m. I was awakened by heavy breathing. I opened my eyes and realised it was Bruno, our overweight labrador.

Once I'd got dressed I went to school with my friend Bill. I told him what had happened and Bill sniggered, 'You really think it's Betsy? Ha! You're barking up the wrong tree there. No, why don't you try Sarah or Nicola?'

'Oh shut up, you, they wouldn't fancy me in a million years. I know it's Betsy but I have to be one hundred per cent sure first,' I told him.

'Why do you think it's Betsy then?' he asked.

'Call it intuition,' I said.

When we got to school the terrible trio (a girly gang looking for mischief) were outside. They were laughing at something and I didn't know what. As I went to the door Lillie said, 'Michael, did you get a Valentine card this year?'

'Yes,' I said, slowly and carefully.

'Did it say who it was from?' Camille squealed.

'No,' I said. My mind, by this time, was ticking over. What if they knew something?

'Why?' I questioned.

'Just asking,' Kathy said in amusement. They went off laughing. I wonder why they said it? Probably doing a survey on Valentine recipients. I went to my lessons.

By lunch time I had two demerits for not doing my homework, two killing feet from sports, and a mind full of questions. Why hasn't anyone owned up yet? Who did it? How long will this annoying puzzle go on for?

Valentine Disaster

The afternoon went quite slowly for me as I had double Physics and Geography. Sarah sat next to me in Physics, but then again, so did Betsy. She was staring at me with gooey eyes, and that annoying drool kept popping out to say hello every five minutes. I swear it's her but the thing is, I don't fancy her. I don't want to hurt her feelings, but I just can't put up with it any longer.

When I got home, Bill was staying over to help me catch up on my homework. How could I do homework at this stage of my investigation?

'I think I know who it is,' Bill stated.

'Who?' I questioned.

'The terrible trio.'

'The terrible trio!' I shouted. 'Of course it's *not* the terrible trio. It's Betsy!'

After that we did our homework and he went home. I had my dinner, then went to bed, ready to face another day in the mysterious world of questions and answers that just need to be united.

Thursday 16th February

Today was different. Today, instead of Bill at the door, it was Betsy asking if I'd like to walk to school with her. I could hardly refuse with my mum towering over me at the time. She had that look on her face. It was saying that if I refused, I would have to do the dishes for a month. I quickly went. As I was walking, Betsy's drool became a pendulum of spit the size of a pencil.

When I got inside the school I breathed a great big sigh of relief. I told myself today is going to be the day that I confront her. I have to remember to talk to her calmly and rationally, and at the same time without hurting her feelings.

At break time I told Bill what I was going to do. He advised me to leave it another week, but I couldn't hold back any longer.

All lunch time I was planning my speech. The trio were in a corner looking at me, laughing and sniggering. All afternoon they were coming up to me and saying things like, 'Have you found your lover yet?' and 'When are you going to tell us who it is?' Why don't they just push off back into their sad, depressing little world and mind their own business?

In Maths we were doing probability. I considered the chances of Betsy either confessing or saying no. I asked Bill and he said, 'The chances of her saying yes are very slim.'

'No, no, more like the other way round,' I replied.

By the last lesson I was dreading having to say it to her face. After school I went to collect my bag. It seemed as if the whole world was watching me. Bill was being very encouraging. I found this didn't help at all. I went up to Betsy gingerly and quietly, hoping she wouldn't notice.

'Hi Michael,' she slobbered.

'Hi Betsy,' I squeaked. Then I went for it. 'Betsy, you really shouldn't have spent your pocket money on a Valentine card, you know.' I said quickly.

'Oh but I wanted to,' she said. 'I *adore* Bill!

Valentine Disaster

He's *so* cute.'

Friday 17th February

Bill is no longer my associate.

One Sorry Night

BY LUCY HAGUE

It begins with the rain. It always begins that way.

The church bells chime. The rain pours down loudly, beating on the gravestones and the railings, and a streetlamp across the road throws cold, white light.

Stark shadows carve out the shape of a boy, kneeling by a gravestone. He turns the dripping page of a book with a chilled hand,

and clears his throat. He reads aloud, over the noise of the rain. When he stops, there is a silence filled only by the sounds of rainfall, nothing else. The streets and roads are empty.

It won't stop raining for hours yet.

He looks at the watery, running ink and lets the book fall shut. He looks at the gravestone he was addressing. And a girl comes out of the darkness, walking cautiously into the circle of light thrown by the streetlamp. She watches him for a long time. He doesn't notice.

'Ingram…?'

He looks up, apparently startled.

'It is you.'

She frowns a little and kneels down beside him.

'What're you doing here at this time of night?'

He shrugs, a little overwhelmed by the sudden presence.

'Um… nothing…'

'I heard you talking. It sounded like you were reading something.'

He shrugs again and nods, looking at the ground.

Her frown deepens, becomes indignant.

'Hey, aren't I good enough for you to talk to or something?'

He says nothing. She stands, scowling impatiently.

'You should be grateful I'm making the effort to speak to you, new boy.'

She looks down at him and gestures to her long, dark hair and pale face.

'I'm the witch, remember? I'm the one who's supposed to be hanging around creepy graveyards on Hallowe'en, not you. So. What're you doing here?'

'Nothing.'

He tightens his grip on the rain-soaked book.

A nasty smile flickers over her face.

'Ah, what have we here? Poetry?'

She kneels beside him and tries to snatch the book away.

'Let me see that!'

He shakes his head violently.

'No... no one sees this, no one...'

'Don't talk to me like that, new boy. I might turn you into a frog.'

Her voice is cold, waiting for a reaction. She shakes her head when none comes.

'God, you're pathetic. I've had better conversations with trees.'

Listen To Me!

She gets to her feet again, about to leave. She sees him looking quietly at the gravestone and hesitates. It's strange. In the graveyard, the new boy, the school geek, looks different. The harsh light cuts hollows in his cheeks and throws shadow into his eyes. The rain runs down his face in rivers of sadness.

She looks at the gravestone but the name is in shadow.

'Is that who you were reading to?'

He looks at the sodden ground.

'Sort of.'

'Did you write it yourself?'

He sighs sadly, nodding again.

'I'm always writing.'

'Yeah, whatever.'

She loses interest and turns to go.

'See you later, new boy.'

The church bells ring out. Midnight.

'Branwen?'

She stops and turns, irritated.

'What?'

'If you're really a witch… can you see the future?'

For a moment she is silent, regarding him stonily.

'Look, I'm not *really* a witch. I'm just interested in the occult.'

She puts her head on one side and frowns at him.

'Why?'

He looks into the distance. The rain-beaten trees are waving in black and white.

'Would you like to see the future?'

She folds her arms and narrows her eyes. Then she shakes her head, sending little droplets of water flying, and speaks seriously.

'No. I think it would make me sad. Because... I'd see all the bad stuff that was going to happen... but I wouldn't be able to change any of it...'

She pauses, and then comes back to life.

'You ask the stupidest questions, new boy. No wonder you haven't got any friends.'

She turns and makes her way back through the dark, looming shapes.

He watches her leave, shaking his head slowly. He listens to the graveyard gate screeching on rusty hinges, her footsteps splashing through the puddles on the pavement. He closes his eyes and turns his face up to the cold rain...

There is a sudden roar of an engine, a scraping squeal of brakes and then wheels skidding on wet tarmac. A high-pitched scream and a thud. Door opening, slamming. Low, slurred voices. Drunks.

Ingram opens his eyes and looks about him, clutching the book to his shivering body. The door slams again. The car backs up, then roars past. The headlights sweep the graveyard, lighting it up, and for a second or two, the writing on the gravestone can be read: Branwen Robert, beloved daughter and sister…

But then the darkness returns, and it's like the writing was never there.

The boy opens the book and stares at the faded, splashed writing. So many more pages, so many more words. So many more apologies to be said…

He looks wearily up into the desolate light

Listen To Me!

of the streetlamp. Then he turns and makes his
way back into the darkness of the graveyard.

Silence falls and the rain beats down.

It always ends that way.

CENTURIES OF STORIES

Edited by Wendy Cooling

Twenty of today's finest authors have each
woven a story around one century. The
result is this unique anthology of
wonderful stories by:

**Michael Morpurgo, Henrietta Branford,
Vivian French, Jean Ure, Robert Swindells,
Mary Hoffman, Annie Dalton, Melvin Burgess,
Gillian Cross, Alan Durant, Theresa Breslin,
Bernard Ashley, Jenny Nimmo, Geraldine
McCaughrean, Pete Johnson, Jacqueline Wilson,
Jeremy Strong, Adèle Geras, Malorie Blackman
and Margaret Mahy.**

'*A splendid collection and a marvellous showcase
for the authors.*' Guardian

'*A terrific, timely celebration of the book.*'
School Librarian

ISBN 0 00 675415 5

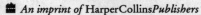

An imprint of HarperCollinsPublishers